97
WAYS TO
TRAIN A DRAGON

By Kate McMullan
Illustrated by Bill Basso

GROSSET & DUNLAP • NEW YORK

For my pal, Jane O'Connor
—K. McM.

Text copyright © 2003 by Kate McMullan. Illustrations copyright © 2003 by Bill Basso. All
rights reserved. Published by Grosset & Dunlap, a division of Penguin Young Readers
Group, 345 Hudson Street, New York, NY 10014. GROSSET & DUNLAP is a trademark of
Penguin Group (USA) Inc. Published simultaneously in Canada. Printed in the U.S.A.

Library of Congress Cataloging-in-Publication Data

McMullan, Kate.
  97 ways to train a dragon / by Kate McMullan ; illustrated by Bill Basso.
     p. cm. — (Dragon Slayers' Academy ; 9)
Summary: After a mysterious egg hatches into a baby dragon, Wiglaf and his roommate
Angus decide to keep it.
  [1. Dragons—Fiction. 2. Schools—Fiction.] I. Title: Ninety-seven ways to train a dragon. II.
Basso, Bill, ill. III. Title.
  PZ7.M2295Aae 2003
  [Fic]—dc22

                              2003017965

ISBN 0-448-43177-7   F G H I J

Chapter I

Wiglaf and Angus raced down the hall-way of Dragon Slayers' Academy. The boys did not want to be late for Dr. Pluck's Dragon Science class. It wasn't because they liked Dragon Science. It was because Dr. Pluck was a spitter. When he said the letter "p," he sprayed the first three rows. So pupils who came late ended up in the Spit Zone.

"Slow down, Wiggie!" Angus panted.

"You don't want to get showered, do you?" Wiglaf put on some speed.

All of a sudden—SPLAT! Wiglaf landed facedown on the cold stone floor.

Angus bent over him. "Are you all right?"

"I—I think so." Wiglaf sat up.

"You fell on that crack. Or maybe one of those." Angus pointed to several. "When my uncle decided to start a school, he bought this old castle for next to nothing because it was falling apart." He pulled Wiglaf to his feet. "I wish he'd at least fix the floors. But that would cost money. And Uncle Mordred hates to part with any of his gold."

By the time the boys walked into the classroom, the only empty seats were in the first three rows. Bragwort, who would do anything to get on a good side of a teacher, sat in the third row. Wiglaf and Angus were about to join him, when Wiglaf caught sight of his friend Erica. She was waving madly.

"Angus!" Wiglaf said. "Erica's saved us seats in the back!"

The two hurried toward her. Erica was always on time for class. It was one reason she won the Future Dragon Slayer of the Month Medal every month. She had also earned nearly every badge offered at DSA. All Wiglaf had was the Dish Washing Badge. Angus had no badges at all. Mordred often said, "If only *all* you boys were like Eric!"

That always made Wiglaf smile. For if all the boys were like Eric, DSA would be a girls' school! How surprised the headmaster would be to learn that Eric was really Princess Erica. Wiglaf and Angus were the only DSA students who knew her true identity.

Wiglaf and Angus slid into the empty seats by Erica.

"Thanks!" they whispered.

Harley Marley sat in the last row, behind Wiglaf. He burped loudly in Wiglaf's ear. Normally Wiglaf wouldn't have taken a seat in front of the school bully. But Wiglaf thought he would rather be burped at than spat upon.

"**Pu**pils! **Pu**pils!" Dr. Pluck rapped his pointer on his desk. "Today we will study dragon young—or **pip**lings, as they are called.

Please, take a **peep** at this **p**icture." He pointed to a chart. Wiglaf saw what looked like a
bird's nest with pink and purple eggs.

"A dragon **prep**ares a nest by digging a **p**it
and **p**utting **p**ine needles in a **p**ile," said Dr.
Pluck. "Then she **p**roduces three eggs. **P**lop!
Plop! **P**lop!" He pointed to the chart. "The
eggs are as **p**lum**p** as pumpkins. Some have
pink s**p**ots and **p**urple s**p**eckles. Some have
pink or **p**urple **p**olka dots. Dragon **p**i**p**lings
peck out of the eggs. **P**op! **P**op! **P**op!" He
flipped over his chart to show three newly
hatched piplings. They were covered in green
egg slime.

Everyone in the class cried, "Ewwwww! "

"I think they're sort of cute," Wiglaf whispered to Angus.

"You would," Angus whispered back.

"Boy **p**i**p**lings have **p**ink ears. Girl **p**i**p**lings'
ears are **p**urple. **P**iplings go 'Peep **p**ee**p** **p**ee**p**!'
Piplings purr. **P**iplings are **p**layful."

~4~

Wiglaf listened while Dr. P sprayed on and on about baby dragons. There were three piplings in every litter. And when a baby dragon opened its eyes, it was love at first sight . . . whoever the pipling saw first (usually the mama dragon) was who it loved best.

Dr. Pluck flipped the chart to show a cleaned-up pipling. It had bright yellow eyes with cherry-red centers, and a little crest on its head. Wiglaf wished he could pick it up.

"Never **p**ick u**p** a **pip**ling!" warned Dr. Pluck. "The first thing a dragon mama teaches her **pip**lings is how to **p**eck, **p**inch, **p**unch, and **p**uff fire. And **pip**ling **p**oo **p**oo? **P**ew!"

"Sir?" Bragwort called. "Can we do extra-credit reports on piplings?"

"**P**erha**p**s," said Dr. Pluck. "Now—"

"Atten-*tion!*" boomed a voice. Headmaster Mordred swept into the room. His red velvet cloak billowed behind him.

"Studying piplings—are you, Pluck?"

said Mordred. "Well, lads! I have some serious news! Sometime before St. Globule's Day, School Inspectors will make a surprise visit to Dragon Slayers' Academy. If this school isn't up to snuff, they will CLOSE ME DOWN!" His booming voice caused the badly cracked ceiling to quiver.

"Look out, sir!" cried Wiglaf as a huge chunk of stone came crashing down, barely missing the headmaster's head.

"Zounds!" cried Mordred, leaping out of the way. He glared up at the hole in the ceiling. "Somebody ought to get that fixed!" He brushed dust from his cloak. "Anyway, I've come to say that all classes are canceled!"

Several boys started to cheer.

"I've canceled classes so you Class I boys can participate in the very first DSA Scrub-a-Thon!"

"Yea!" cried Harley Marley, who wasn't paying attention.

"The Class II and III boys are in charge of

fixing and patching," Mordred said. "You Class I lads get to clean, sweep, mop, dust, wash, scrape, scour, polish, shine, and scrub *everything!*" said Mordred. "DSA *will* pass inspection!"

All the pupils groaned. Even Erica.

"And if you see anyone goofing off?" Mordred added. "Come and whisper in my ear. Enough little whispers, and you know what you'll earn?"

"The Tattle-Tale Badge," called Bragwort.

"Yes!" said Mordred. "A beautiful yellow badge it is, too."

Wiglaf didn't want the Tattle Tale Badge. It was one of the few badges that Erica did not have stitched to her tunic.

"Now, lads, here is a new badge," Mordred held up a black patch with pink letters: D.P. "I need volunteers for a very special assignment."

Wiglaf and Angus slid down in their seats.

They knew better than to take a "special assignment" from Mordred.

"I need boys," Mordred continued, "to pick up all the junk that I dumped—er, I mean, that someone dumped from the DSA castle to the banks of Swamp River!"

Wiglaf and Angus slunk so far down that they were practically on the floor.

"Whoever I pick must be back at DSA by breakfast time," Mordred added. "That way they can join in the scrubbing with everybody else."

"I'll go!" called Erica.

"Not you, Eric," Mordred said. "I have a special scrubbing job for you." His plum-colored eyes bounced from boy to boy. Wiglaf did not allow himself to breathe.

Just then Wiglaf felt a tickle on the back of his neck. Behind him, Harley Marley snickered. Wiglaf tried to brush whatever it was away. It felt . . . furry. Yikes! It was a hairy spider! The spider clamped its jaws down on

Wiglaf's finger.

"YAAAAAAA!" shrieked Wiglaf. He jumped up, shaking his hand to rid it of the spider. The thing was the size of a guinea pig!

"Ah ha!" Mordred called. "A volunteer!" He pointed at Wiglaf, who had finally managed to shake off the spider.

Harley Marley snorted with laughter.

"Wiglaf and who else?" Mordred's eyes lit on the boy sitting next to Wiglaf. "Nephew!" he cried. "All you do around here is eat my food! You need exercise!"

"No, uncle!" Angus begged. "Not that!"

The headmaster grinned. "And you shall get it running to Swamp River tomorrow morning, picking up trash! Get your trash bags in the gatehouse at IV:00 a.m.! Nephew! You and Wiglaf are the very first members of Dawn Patrol!"

Chapter 2

Wiglaf opened one eye. He squinted at Erica's glow-in-the-dark hourglass perched on the ledge. Quarter to IV.

"Angus?" Wiglaf said. "Are you awake?"

"No," Angus groaned. "I'm sound asleep having a horrible nightmare that I'm out in the freezing cold picking up trash!"

Wiglaf stayed under his blanket as he pulled on his tunic. Once Angus was dressed, his pockets filled with snacks, the boys tiptoed out of the DSA castle. By the gate house, they found a stack of burlap bags. They picked them up, pushed open the big wooden DSA gates, and walked over the creaky drawbridge into the moonlit night.

Wiglaf took a breath of night air. "Ugh!" he said, nearly choking. "What reeks?"

"Frypot must have thrown out more left-overs," said Angus.

Frypot, the DSA cook, served leftovers night after night. Only when a Fried Eel Casserole or Jellied Eel Surprise began to turn green and foam around the edges did he finally toss it out the kitchen window onto his garbage heap.

The boys walked quickly to escape the ghastly smell. On and on they trudged. The sky was turning pink by the time they reached the Swamp River. It was light enough for Wiglaf to see that the riverbank was littered with candle stubs, old boots, rusted armor parts, chicken bones, and too many empty mead bottles to count.

"I need a rest," said Angus.

"We haven't even started yet," said Wiglaf.

Angus sat on a rock and closed his eyes.

Wiglaf grabbed a bag. He began walking and tossing in trash. Soon his bag was bulging.

"One bag filled," Wiglaf reported to Angus.

"Good work!" said Angus.

Wiglaf sighed and started off in the other direction. Then, without warning, he skidded on something slippery. His feet slid out from under him, and he fell off a small ledge. Plop! He landed on something soft. Slowly, he sat up. He shook his head. He wasn't hurt. But he was sitting in a puddle of nasty green slime!

"Angus!" Wiglaf called. "Help!"

Angus lumbered over. He peered down at Wiglaf.

"Get me out of here, Angus," said Wiglaf. He held up a slimy green hand.

Angus drew back. "Ooh, yuck!" Then he frowned. "Wiggie, you're sitting in a nest."

"I am?" Wiglaf looked around. Yes. He was in a nest—a nest with bits of eggshells in it.

Pink and purple eggshells. He remembered what Dr. Pluck had said. Dragon eggs were pink or purple. And newly hatched piplings were covered in green slime. Wiglaf's eyes widened. "I think I am sitting on a dragon's nest, Angus. And look! There's an unhatched dragon egg!"

Angus jumped down into the pit. He and Wiglaf bent over the deep purple egg. It was the size of a small pumpkin.

"A dragon egg." Angus stared at it. "Are you thinking what I'm thinking, Wiggie?"

"Yes!" said Wiglaf.

Angus grinned. "Scrambled dragon egg!"

"No!" cried Wiglaf. "That's not what I'm thinking! Angus, the egg—it's *warm*! This egg could still hatch—into a little pipling!"

"I bet it's a dud," said Angus. "Or it would have hatched with the others. Anyway, you heard what Dr. Pluck said. Dragon piplings are really nasty."

"He said mama dragons teach their piplings to peck and pinch and punch," Wiglaf said. "Maybe they're born nice. We could find out. Let's take the egg back."

"You've lost your mind," said Angus.

"We can't leave it here to hatch," said Wiglaf. "It's all alone. And think of it, Angus. We could raise a little pet pipling! Come on, Angus. Don't you like animals?"

"I love animals!" said Angus. "But animals don't like me."

"How can you say that?" asked Wiglaf.

"'Tis true," said Angus. "Your pet pig, Daisy, stays away from me."

"Only when you say how much you love bacon," Wiglaf said.

"When I go to the henhouse," Angus said, "the hens run in fear."

"Only when you start talking about drumsticks," said Wiglaf.

"My mother bought me a goldfish once,"

Angus said. "Every time I looked at him, he dove under a plant to hide."

"You just haven't found the right pet yet," said Wiglaf. "Maybe it's a pipling! Come on, Angus. Help me take this egg back to DSA."

Wiglaf wrapped burlap bags around the egg. Angus held another bag open and Wiglaf slipped the wrapped-up egg inside. Then the boys started back to school.

"Yikes!" said Angus. "Look! Uncle Mordred's on the drawbridge, waiting for us!"

Wiglaf gently lowered the bag with the egg inside. He began dragging it as if it were no more than a bag of trash.

The boys stopped at the top of the small hill in front of the drawbridge.

"Hello, Uncle," said Angus.

"What? So few bags?" Mordred bellowed. "You lazy lads!"

Suddenly, the bag with the egg inside wobbled and began rolling down the hill. Wiglaf dove for it.

"What's inside that bag, boy?"

"Um . . . . the usual, sir," said Wiglaf.

Mordred's violet eyes lit up. "You caught a swamp wog didn't you, boys? Ohh, I love a roasted swamp wog. You're trying to sneak it by me so you can have it all to yourselves!"

"No, sir!" said Wiglaf. "I—I have never even seen a swamp wog!"

"Don't lie to me, boy!" boomed Mordred. "Bring me the bag!"

Wiglaf froze.

"You can have this bag, Uncle!" Angus picked up his bag—by the wrong end. He swung it over his shoulder and all the trash flew out, spraying Mordred with chicken bones, old boots, and mead bottles. "Oops! Sorry, Uncle!" called Angus.

"Nephew!" Mordred roared as the boys took off running. "You're fired! You, too,

Wiglaf! No Dawn Patrol badges for you!"

Wiglaf and Angus broke into smiles as they ran. No more Dawn Patrol!

Once in the front door at DSA, the boys hurried up the stairs, past unlucky fellow students on their hands and knees, scrubbing the steps.

On the second floor, they scurried down DSA's Hall of Fame. They ran past the statues of the DSA founders, Sir Herbert Dungeonstone and Sir Ichabod Popquizz. Past marble statues of famous knights and the famous dragons they had slain. Past a life-sized bust of Mordred. The scent in the Hall of Fame reminded Wiglaf of some happy moment from his childhood. But what? He never could remember.

At the end of the hallway, Wiglaf caught sight of Erica. She was scrubbing bold black letters off the wall:

HELP! I AM BEING HELD PRISONER

BEHIND THIS WALL!

Just a joke, Wiglaf hoped.

On they rushed, past Bragwort, who was cleaning a rusty drinking fountain.

"No fair!" Bragwort called after them. "Why aren't you scrubbing?"

"We're on Dawn Patrol, remember?" said Angus. "And we have to get rid of this trash bag."

"Whew!" said Angus when at last they reached the dorm room. "No one's here."

Wiglaf carried the egg over to his cot. He took it out of its bag so he could look again at its deep purple color.

"Hello, in there, pipling!" Wiglaf whispered. Then he turned to Angus. "Can I hide it under your cot? You've got so much stuff under there, no one will notice an egg."

"If it hatches, all my clothes will get

slimed," said Angus.

"Hatching takes a long time," said Wiglaf. "Even if the pipling begins pecking on the shell, we'll be back before it hatches."

"Oh, all right." Angus fell to his knees and began digging out tunics, leggings, under-shirts, and socks from under his cot.

Wiglaf wrapped the egg in Angus's dirty laundry. Then he slid it back under Angus's cot.

"Don't hatch, pipling," said Wiglaf. "At least not yet."

Chapter 3

By the time the boys ran into the dining hall, it was empty.

"You've missed breakfast," said Frypot the cook. "Lucky for you I've still got some eel-meal." He handed them steaming bowls of hot cereal.

Wiglaf stared at the quivering gray lump. Even Angus turned up his nose. "Is there nothing else?"

In the end, they choked it down. Then they went off to scrub alongside their classmates. As he scrubbed, Wiglaf thought about the purple egg. He wondered what the little pipling inside might look like. Would it peep? Would it have tiny wings?

By the time Angus and Wiglaf and some other boys staggered back to the dorm room that night, they were too tired to think.

Angus threw himself fully dressed onto his cot. Two seconds later, he was snoring.

Wiglaf, however, sat on his cot. He wanted to look at the egg. He wanted to see if the pipling had started pecking. But he would have to wait until all the other boys were asleep. He was pulling off his boots when Erica came in.

"Wiggie!" she said happily. "The carpet I ordered from the Sir Lancelot catalog arrived!"

Wiglaf followed her over to her bunk on the far side of the dorm. She already had a Sir Lancelot tapestry hanging above her cot. And now beside her cot was a small carpet woven with a likeness of a fully-armored Sir Lancelot.

"Very nice," Wiglaf told her. He wished he could tell her about the dragon egg. But

Bragwort might overhear. He didn't want to risk it.

"That's not all," Erica went on. "Mordred put me on Dawn Patrol."

"Congratulations!" Wiglaf saw that she had already sewn the DP badge onto her tunic.

"Bragwort is the other member of Dawn Patrol," she added. "But Mordred made me captain! I must get right to sleep. Good night, Wiggie."

"Good night," Wiglaf answered. He went back to his cot and lay down under his thin, thread-bare blanket.

After torches out, Wiglaf let his eyes get used to the dim light. When he felt sure everyone was asleep, he knelt down beside Angus's cot and pulled out the laundry nest. He uncovered the egg. It was still warm. He felt for cracks in the shell, but found none.

"Not ready to hatch yet, are you pipling?" Wiglaf whispered.

Then he lifted his own thin blanket and put the egg down at the foot of his cot. Ahhh. It felt good, having a warm egg on his cold feet.

Wiglaf closed his eyes. He was glad Scrub-a-Thon was over. But could DSA really pass inspection? Wiglaf didn't think so. Not unless the inspectors had bad eyes. And stuffy noses.

Tat-tat! Tat-tat!

The noise woke Wiglaf from a deep sleep. He sat up.

Tat-tat!

There it was again!

Tat-tat-tat-tat-tat-tat-tat!

Suddenly, it hit him. The egg! It was hatching!

Tat-tat-tat-tat!

A dim glow lit the room. Holding her mini-torch, Erica padded over to his cot.

TAT-TAT-TAT-TAT-TAT-TAT-TAT!

"Wiggie?" she whispered. "What's that?"

"Sit down, Erica," Wiglaf whispered back. "I have something to tell you."

"You are joking!" Erica said when she had heard all about the purple egg.

TAT-TAT-TAT!

"No joke." Wiglaf pulled back his blanket. The egg now had crack lines all over it.

PECK!

Wiglaf and Erica jumped back as a head popped out of the egg. A circle of purple shell sat atop it like a hat. The pipling had a long neck. And a little snout. Its eyes were shut.

"A pipling!" breathed Erica.

"Pink ears," whispered Wiglaf. "It's a boy!"

The pipling yawned. Wiglaf thought he had never seen anything so cute. He reached out a hand to touch it. But before he could, the little dragon ducked back into its shell.

Then *Boing!* A clawed foot poked through the bottom of the egg.

Boing! Another foot.

Boing! Boing! Two clawed front paws.

The little head popped out again. The dragon was half in and half out of the purple shell.

"Hello, pipling," Wiglaf whispered.

The little dragon turned its head toward the sound of his voice. But his eyes stayed shut.

Just then Angus groaned in his sleep.

The noise startled the pipling. With a chirp, he ducked inside its egg again.

"Wha—?" Angus opened one eye and caught sight of the half-hatched pipling. He sat up, wide awake now. He gasped. "Sir Lancelot's liver!"

"Shhhh!" Wiglaf said. "You'll wake the whole dorm."

The pipling's head popped up again. With one last push, his tail broke through the egg. Now a whole baby dragon sat at the end of Wiglaf's cot. It wasn't as slimy as the

piplings in Dr. Pluck's picture. It was no bigger than a little bunny.

"Amazing!" Angus breathed.

"Adorable," Wiglaf added.

"Against the rules!" Erica reminded them.

"Not really," said Wiglaf. "Where does it say dragon eggs can't hatch in the dorm?"

The pipling took two wobbly steps. Then he fell back on his little bum.

"His first steps!" said Wiglaf proudly.

"Listen," said Erica. "I'm on Dawn Patrol. I'll take him back to his nest."

"You can't!" said Wiglaf. "No one is there to take care of him."

"Right!" said Angus. "And he wouldn't have anything to eat."

Just then the pipling picked up his head and cried: "Wrrrrrm!"

"Worm?" Wiglaf laughed. "Is that your name? Worm?"

Angus grinned. "Hello, Worm."

"Wrrrrm!" the pipling replied. "Wrrrrm! Wrrrrm! Wrrrrm!"

Worm opened his mouth and stuck out his forked tongue.

"He's hungry!" Angus said. "I'll get him something from my stash."

Wiglaf and Erica perked up when they heard this. Angus's stash was famous. His mother sent him tins of goodies each week. But Angus never shared. Until now.

Angus turned to the wall beside his cot. He pressed one end of a loose stone and lifted it out. Wiglaf and Erica gasped. So that's where he hid it! Angus took out a bag of Medieval Marshmallows.

"Don't tell," said Angus. He handed them each a marshmallow.

Wiglaf watched the little dragon down on the floor.

"Here, little Worm," Angus called, holding out a marshmallow.

Without opening his eyes, the pipling snatched the treat out of Angus's hand.

"He likes it!" said Angus. He gave him another marshmallow. And another.

"Not too many," said Erica.

"After all, he was just born," said Wiglaf.

The pipling hopped toward Angus. He waited for another marshmallow.

"He likes me!" said Angus. He picked up the pipling.

"Dr. Pluck said not to do that!" Erica warned.

Suddenly, the pipling opened his little mouth and *bleaaach!* Angus's tunic was covered in warm marshmallow spit up.

"Oh, well," said Angus. He picked up a dirty sock and mopped up the urp. "He's only a baby. I wonder what we should feed him."

Wiglaf smiled. Worm had fallen fast asleep with his head resting on Angus's tummy. He looked so comfortable, just the way Wiglaf felt when he snuggled against the big unicorn pillow in the library.

"We have to get him out of here," said Erica. "What if the inspectors were to show up and find him? They'd shut down DSA."

"We'll hide him," Angus whispered.

"Are you crazy?" said Erica. "He shall grow up to be a fire-breathing monster!"

"Hey, what's going on here?" Bragwort sat up on his cot.

"Yikes! Bragwort!" Erica clicked off her torch.

Wiglaf quickly tossed his blanket over Angus's lap, hoping to hide the pipling.

"I heard a noise," said Bragwort. "You're hiding something. I can tell."

"As Class I Dorm Monitor, I order you back to sleep, Bragwort!" said Erica.

"I shall figure out what you're hiding, Eric," Bragwort said. "And I shall tell Mordred! Then I'll be Future Dragon Slayer of the

Month, not you."

"Oh, go blow your nose!" said Erica.

"I will," said Bragwort. "All over your Sir Lancelot carpet!"

Wiglaf waited until he could hear snuffling snores from Bragwort. Then he whispered, "We do have to get Worm out of here."

Angus said, "But where?"

"Perhaps the henhouse," Wiglaf answered, "No one goes there. I'll ask Daisy to look after him." He turned to Erica. "You won't tell anyone about the pipling, will you?"

"What pipling?" said Erica. "I never saw any pipling." She headed back to her cot.

Wiglaf threw on his tunic. Angus had no need to, for he had slept in his. Then, with the sleeping pipling wrapped in his blanket, Wiglaf and Angus tiptoed out of the dorm.

Chapter 4

"Daisy?" Wiglaf whispered as he crept into the henhouse. "Are you awake, girl?"

"Es-yay," came Daisy's voice. Wiglaf's pig spoke Pig Latin ever since a wizard cast a spell on her.

"We have a problem, Daisy," said Wiglaf. "His name is Worm." And he quickly told her the story.

"Could you look after him, Daisy?" asked Angus.

"E-may?" Daisy looked alarmed.

"We'll bring food for him later," Wiglaf told her. "Worm'll be safe here. Bragwort is suspicious . . . he's sure to tell Mordred on us."

"O-kay!" said Daisy. She rooted around in

her straw and made a place for the pipling.

As the boys left they heard Daisy singing softly, "Inkle-tway, inkle-tway, ittle-lay ar-stay . . . "

"Angus!" Wiglaf stopped suddenly. "I know how we can figure out what Worm likes to eat —the library!"

"You think he eats books?" said Angus.

"No!" said Wiglaf. "We'll find a book about baby dragons!"

So the boys headed for the south tower. By the time they had run up the hundreds of crumbling steps to the top, Angus was gasping for breath.

The library was the only place in the whole school with great big windows. On a sunny day, light flooded in. Even this early, Wiglaf could see a wide stretch of rosy sky.

Brother Dave, the DSA librarian, had made the library most inviting. He'd put a huge unicorn pillow on the floor for students to lie on while they read. He'd put posters on the walls. One showed a knight wearing a book for armor. He was knocking another knight off his horse. A caption read, <u>You can't beat a book.</u> The trouble was, most DSA students didn't even know their school had a library.

"Brother Dave?" Wiglaf called.

"Cometh in!" the DSA librarian called.

"Ah, 'tis thou, Wiglaf," the monk said with a smile. "A visit to the library. A fine way to begin thy day. Bless me! Here is Angus, too!"

"Brother Dave," said Angus, "we need a book on raising baby dragons."

Brother Dave tapped a finger on his chin. "Waitest here." The monk toddled off toward the shelves in the back of the library. A moment later, he emerged from the stacks. He was covered in cobwebs. "Thou art in luck," he said, putting a small dusty book into his hands.

Angus blew dust from the book. There were fancy gold letters on the cover.

"*97 Ways to Train Your Dragon*," Angus read, "by Sir Sitstayheel." He flopped down on the big unicorn pillow, opened the little book and began reading aloud:

> *Congratulations! You have a new dragon pipling. (If you don't, why in the world are you reading this book?)*
>
> *A newly hatched pipling can't see. It can't walk, either. But soon it will enter the 'bouncing stage.' It will bounce higher and higher, and then one day it will spread its pipling wings and take off.*

Angus kept flipping pages. "Feeding!"

> *Never feed your pipling marshmallows. If you do, he will throw up all over your tunic.*

"Too bad we didn't know that before," said Angus and he read on:

> *In the wild, a mama dragon chews up eels and feeds them to her piplings. You must also feed your pipling *ABC Eel.*
>
> *(*ABC = Already Been Chewed.)*

Angus made a face and read on:

Piplings like raw eel. The first few chews are disgusting. But you'll get used to it.

"Ugh!" said Wiglaf. "I can't do that."

"Me, neither," said Angus. He looked back down at the book.

All right, if you can't, you can't. Used cooked eel, then. But you MUST chew it up.

"We do that three times a day in the dining hall," said Angus.

Brother Dave chuckled. "How happy it makest me to see lads who love learning!"

"Thanks for finding this book, Brother Dave," said Angus.

"Thou art welcome, Angus," said Brother Dave. "Cometh back soon."

Yesterday Wiglaf and Angus had been too late for breakfast. But today they made it just in time. They picked up trays and slid them along the railings.

Angus plopped an extra-large helping of

Scrambled Eel onto his plate.

Wiglaf helped himself to extra Creamed Eel on Toast. It looked nasty. He wondered if the pipling would like it.

The boys sat down at the Class I table. Angus kept reading as he shoveled in his breakfast.

> *Piplings can be fussy eaters. But all piplings love moat weed, moat slime, moat sludge, moat scum, moat eels, and knights.*

As he listened, Wiglaf slipped some creamed eels into his tunic pocket.

"A book?" Bragwort said, eyeing Angus. "You know how to read?"

"Your own business, Bragwort," said Angus. "Mind it."

"Give it here," said Bragwort. He grabbed for the book.

But before he could get his hands on it, the headmaster strode into the dining hall.

"Atten-*tion!*" he called.

All the boys jumped up.

"Scrub-a-Thon is off to a good start! But I need this school as clean and shiny as a newly minted gold coin!" Mordred's eyes glazed over, as his thoughts turned to riches.

At that moment, a large bear lumbered into the dining hall.

Bragwort screamed. "Sir! Bear attack! Bear attack!"

Mordred quickly picked up his chair and started swinging.

"My lord! Stop!" cried the bear, ducking as the chair whizzed over his head. "'Tis I, your scout, Yorick!"

Mordred stopped mid-swing. "Yorick?" He lowered the chair. "What news, Yorick?"

"The inspectors have just left Dragon Stabbers' Prep, my lord," said Yorick. "That school lost points for its dirty kitchen."

"Well, they won't find any dirt in the DSA kitchen!" said Mordred.

"Guess where we'll be scrubbing today," whispered Angus.

"I will give Scrub-a-Thon badges to boys doing a super-duper job!" Mordred finished.

A few of the newer boys clapped weakly. Mordred strode out of the dining hall.

Within the hour, Wiglaf stood next to Angus, working on eel-encrusted skillets and cauldrons coated with boar grease. They had just enough time to dash to the henhouse before lunch.

"How's Worm doing, Daisy?" asked Angus.

"O-say ute-cay!" said Daisy. She wiped eel juice from Worm's chin.

"*Wwwwwwwrm!*" purred the pipling.

Wiglaf smiled. He'd never seen Daisy look happier. Or Angus, either.

Over the next few days, Wiglaf and Angus dashed from their Scrub-a-Thon chores to the henhouse whenever they could. Angus took charge of feeding the little dragon. Worm was always hungry. But since Frypot served eel at every meal, bringing eel tidbits for the little dragon was no problem. And the dragon was growing bigger every day.

Daisy loved the little pipling. Her only complaint was the pipling's "inky-stay oop-pay." And the hens didn't seem to mind having a pipling in their house. He stayed in Daisy's stall and out of their way.

One morning when the boys arrived, Daisy held Worm up.

"Ook-lay!" she said.

"Oh! He got his first fang!" said Angus. "I wonder when he'll open his eyes." He took the pipling from Daisy and put him down on the ground. "Such a good little fellow!"

But the next morning when the boys opened the henhouse door, dozens of hens burst out, cackling and squawking.

"Daisy?" Wiglaf called, running toward her stall. "Daisy!"

"Is Worm all right?" cried Angus.

The pig was hunkered down in a corner. The pipling was bouncing all over the henhouse like a crazy rubber ball.

"Looks like he's hit the bouncing stage," said Wiglaf. "Worm, come to me."

The pipling turned blindly and bounced toward Wiglaf's voice. *Boing! Boing!* He bounced right into Wiglaf's arms. Angus held up a small chunk of scrambled eel.

Worm lifted his head. He sniffed. Then *slurp!* The eel was gone.

While Angus fed Worm, Daisy told Wiglaf that when the pipling woke up, he started bouncing and nothing would stop him.

"All gone, Worm," Angus said at last.

"*Wrrrrrrm!*" said Worm. Tiny twin flames spurted out of his nose.

"He's still hungry," said Angus.

"Can I try to feed him?" Wiglaf asked.

"All right." Angus folded his arms across his

chest. "But only a little, okay? You have Daisy. I want Worm to like me best."

Wiglaf dangled an eel in front of Worm's nose. Worm sniffed. *Slurp!* Then he opened his mouth. *Burp!*

Wiglaf laughed. He tickled the pipling under the chin.

Suddenly Worm's eyes popped open. Yellow eyes, with cherry-red centers. Worm tilted his head. He kept looking at Wiglaf. He almost seemed to be smiling.

"Angus!" said Wiglaf as he wiggled the eel. "Worm's eyes just opened!"

Angus rushed over. "He can see me now! Come to me, Worm!" called Angus, patting his lap. "Here, boy!"

But Worm kept his gaze on Wiglaf. He blinked again. Then he opened his little pink mouth and warbled, "*Mmmmmmmommy!*"

Chapter 5

"I'm sorry, Angus, truly, I am," said Wiglaf as the boys hurried back to the castle for more Scrub-a-Thon. "I never meant for Worm to see me as his . . . mommy."

They had left Worm in the henhouse, in his nest, tired from all his boinging. Daisy agreed to look after him, but warned Wiglaf that he was getting to be too much for his "ig-pay anny-nay."

"It's not your fault that Worm loves you best, Wiggie," said Angus glumly as they reached the kitchen. "Animals love you. It's just that Worm was really starting to like me."

"It was only luck," said Wiglaf. "If Worm had seen you when he opened his eyes, he'd be calling you Mmmmommy. Don't give up on Worm, Angus. He does love you. I can tell."

"You think?" said Angus.

Frypot was handing out buckets of soapy water and scrub brushes.

"You two are to scrub the statues in the DSA Hall of Fame," Frypot said. He leaned over and added in a whisper, "Mordred saves pennies where he can, you know, and he's the one who paid for those statues. I wouldn't scrub 'em too hard if I was you, lads."

Angus and Wiglaf lugged their heavy buckets up the stairs. They stopped in front of the dust-encrusted statues of the DSA founders.

"I will scrub Sir Herbert Dungeonstone," said Wiglaf.

"Then I will scrub Sir Ichabod Popquizz," said Angus.

And they started in. But as he cleaned Sir Herbert's dirty face, it seemed to Wiglaf that his brush grew sudsier and sudsier. And—what was that smell? He had smelled something like this once, years ago. But, what? It seemed to Wiglaf that Sir Herbert's nose was smaller than it had been. Egad! How was that possible?

"Lancelot's liver!" cried Angus from across the hallway. "I have scrubbed off Sir Ichabod's ear!"

Wiglaf felt Sir Herbert's face. It wasn't hard, like marble. It felt soft. Like...what?

"Uncle Mordred is such a cheapskate!" cried Angus. "These statues aren't marble. They're carved out of soap!"

Soap! It all came flooding back to Wiglaf. He had smelled soap the time his father had gone off to buy a new pig trough and his mother had given him and his twelve brothers a bath!

Angus pinched a bit of soap together and molded a new ear for Sir Ichabod.

"It doesn't look quite like the old ear, does it?" he said.

Wiglaf looked, and saw that this was true.

"Well, it's the best I can do," Angus said. Then he added, "Wiglaf, what if Worm didn't see you for a while? Do you think he might forget about you?"

"Maybe," said Wiglaf, though he hoped it wasn't true.

"Maybe if Worm sees me, just me," Angus went on, "he'll start to like me best."

"Maybe," said Wiglaf.

"So why don't I go check on him?" said Angus. "Just me."

Wiglaf nodded. "Go on. I'll take back your bucket." He watched Angus hurry down the Hall of Fame. It didn't seem fair. After all, he was the one who'd wanted to hatch a pipling. But if staying away helped Worm and Angus get closer, then he guessed it was worth it.

Wiglaf finished washing Sir Herbert's boots. Then he picked up the buckets. He was on his way to take them to Frypot when Angus came running down the hall waving wildly.

"Wiggie!" Angus cried. "It's Worm! He's gone!"

Wiglaf dropped both buckets. "But where could he go?"

"Daisy tried to tell me," said Angus. "But I can't understand her, Wiggie. Help!"

Back at the henhouse, Daisy told Wiglaf exactly what had happened.

"E-hay ounced-bay out-yay e-thay ack-bay oor-day," cried Daisy. "En-thay I-yay eard-hay a-yay ash-splay."

"Worm bounced out the back door of the henhouse," Wiglaf told Angus. "And then Daisy heard a splash."

"He's fallen into the moat!" cried Angus. "Come on, Wiggie! We've got to save him!"

But just then Wiglaf heard *"Mmmmommy!"* And there was Worm, bouncing toward them. *Boing! Boing! Boing!*

The hens screeched and scattered as the

pipling bounded around the henhouse. He was soaking wet. Pieces of moat grass clung to his scales. Wiglaf thought he was bigger than he'd been just that morning.

"*Mmmmommy!*" purred Worm. He nuzzled Wiglaf. Then—*Bam!*—he butted his head into his stomach.

"Oof!" Wiglaf grunted. "He's strong!"

Next Worm bounced toward Daisy. *Boing! Boing!* But the pig had had enough. She shot out of the henhouse. Wiglaf saw that she was trotting in the direction of the library.

The pipling bounced back to Wiglaf. *Boing! Boing! Boing!*

"Get the book out, Angus!" cried Wiglaf. "We have to train him!"

Angus pulled *97 Ways to Train Your Dragon* from his pocket.

"You do it," he said. "He'll do better if someone he likes trains him." He began to read:

Training begins the moment a pipling is hatched. Training is more than just saying, "No! Stop! Ow! That really hurts!" Training is a way of becoming friends with your pipling. (Being a "friend" will become important later, when your pipling turns into a giant fire-breathing monster, who can easily bite your head off, set you on fire, and pick up what's left of you in its claws and carry you off to its cave where it will . . . wait a minute, where was I?

Still, training a dragon pipling can be fun. All it takes is patience, practice, and getting used to pain.

Follow these steps, from 1 to 97, and dragon training can be safe, too. Well, not safe, exactly. But you might live through it.

Way #1: The best time to train your pipling is when he is hungry. (But not too hungry.)

Way #2: Keep that First Aid Kit handy.

Way #3: Buy a super-sized tub of Burn Ointment.

Way #4: Never turn your back on your pipling.

Way #5: Never show fear.

Wiglaf thought Sir Sitstayheel made training sound scary. He darted a look at Worm. Yikes! The pipling was shooting flames from his nose. In a minute he would set the straw on fire!

"Worm, stop!" cried Wiglaf. He scooped Worm up and held him. The pipling began licking his cheek. "Is there anything on how to stop him from setting things on fire?"

Angus flipped some pages. "Warnings, warnings," he muttered, flipping page after page. "Ah, here it is."

Way # 28: Flaming.

Most piplings like to blow flames out their snouts. It makes them feel powerful.

Ask yourself: Can I turn this scary behavior into something good?

My answer is: Yes!

Show your pipling how to light the candles on your dining table.

Let him light your cigar.

Let him toast your marshmallows. (But don't give him one.)

To get him started, say, "Flame on!" When you want him to stop, look him in the eyes and say, "Flame out!"

If you can't get your pipling to look at you, go to Way # 29: Eye Contact.

"Okay," said Wiglaf. Eye contact. That sounded like something he could do.

Way # 29: Face your pipling.

Wiglaf put Worm down. He faced him.

Hold an eel treat to his nose.

Wiglaf dug an eel from his pocket. He held it up in front of Worm.

(If you are right handed, use your left hand —in case the worst should happen. Lefties, use your right.)

Wiglaf quickly switched hands.

Now pull the treat from your pipling's nose directly to your eyes.

Wiglaf was about to pull the eel treat toward his eyes when—*Slurp!* The eel disappeared.

Wiglaf tried again. *Slurp!* The same thing happened.

Angus checked the book. "Ah," he said. "Listen to this."

Did your pipling slurp up the eel right away? If so, go directly to Way #30.

Way #30: As the trainer of a dragon pipling, YOU must have the right attitude. YOU are in charge! YOU are in control. YOU are the boss! It is all up to YOU! Now make that pipling behave.

Wiglaf nodded. "I'm in charge, Worm," he said. He tried to sound stern.

"*Mmmmmmommy!*" Worm burbled.

"Oh, Worm!" Wiglaf laughed. "You are so funny!"

"*Mmmmmmommy! Mmmmmmommy!*" Worm snatched another eel treat. *Slurp!*

Angus put the book down. "Wiglaf, you are hopeless!" he said.

Wiglaf nodded. "I'm just not the bossy type."

"Here." Angus handed Wiglaf the book. "Let me try."

But before Angus could dig an eel out of his pocket, Worm bounced off toward the back of the henhouse.

"Worm, stop!" cried Angus.

The boys chased after the little dragon who wriggled through a sizable hole in the castle wall.

The boys wriggled through the hole, too. On the other side, Wiglaf put up a hand to shade his eyes from the sun. He looked in the moat. "I don't see him, do you?"

"No. But here comes Uncle Mordred! I hope he doesn't see him either!"

Chapter 6

Wiglaf and Angus flattened themselves against a curve in the castle wall. They watched Mordred walk quickly toward the rear of the castle.

"Must be checking on his trash pit," said Angus.

Wiglaf kept his eyes on the moat. He saw a small head pop up out of the water. Worm! The pipling had an eel hanging out of his mouth. He threw back his head and gulped it down. Then he flapped his wings, splashing like crazy.

"Who goes there?" Mordred cried. His violet eyes looked up and down the moat. But the pipling had dived back under the water.

Only when Mordred walked off did Wiglaf start to breathe again.

"There's Worm!" cried Angus. "Wiggie, we have to save him!" He grabbed Wiglaf by the arm and before Wiglaf knew what was happening—SPLASH!—he and Angus hit the water.

Brrrr! It was freezing! Wiglaf surfaced. He swiped the moat weeds from his head with one hand while he paddled with the other.

"I see him!" cried Angus. "Come on!"

Wiglaf swam after Angus toward Worm.

Only the pipling's skinny little neck and head stuck out of the water. He saw the boys coming and burbled happily. "*Wrrrrrm!*"

Angus reached out for the pipling.

Worm's eyes lit up, and he dove under the water again.

Wiglaf groaned. "He thinks it's a game, Angus."

"Ahoy, lads!" came a voice.

Wiglaf looked up. On the bank of the moat

stood Coach Plungett, the DSA gym teacher.

"Practicing your swimming strokes, I see!" Coach said.

"Jolly good! Glad to see you getting some exercise, Angus. And Wiglaf, more reach with those arms." He began demonstrating the crawl stroke.

The boys swam using their best form.

"Better!" shouted Coach. "Much better!"

Just then Worm popped up again.

Coach had one arm up over his head. He didn't see the pipling.

"Like this, lads!" called Coach Plungett. "Do this every day, and you'll grow up to be manly men, like me!"

"*Wrrrrrm! Wrrrrrrm!*" Worm called to Wiglaf and Angus.

Coach was busy demonstrating the frog kick on land. "With lads like you on the swim team, we'll beat Dragon Stabbers Prep, or my name isn't Wendell Plungett!" Coach cried.

"Well, I must go and meet my sweet Belcheena for lunch. Farewell!" He waved and strode off toward the cottage on Huntsman's Path where he lived with his bride.

As Wiglaf waved back, Worm sprang up right in front of him. He was slurping down another eel. Wiglaf threw his arms around him. But the slippery pipling slid out of his grasp.

"Come, Worm," Wiglaf coaxed. "Come to Mommy!"

"*Mmmmmmmmmmommy!*" said Worm. He swam to Wiglaf. But as Wiglaf reached for him, he darted away. He did this again and again.

Meanwhile, Angus swam quietly up behind the pipling and began treading water.

"Worm! Look at me!" Angus ordered.

Worm turned around.

Angus didn't reach for him. He stuck out his chin. He flared his nostrils. He did not blink as he stared at the little dragon.

Worm cocked his head as if trying to decide

whether Angus meant business.

Angus kept his gaze on Worm as he slowly brought his arm out of the water. He had an eel in his hand. He held it to the pipling's nose.

Worm looked at it cross-eyed, but did not snap it up.

Slowly, Angus drew the eel treat toward his own eyes.

And there it was—eye contact!

"You may have the treat now, Worm," said Angus. He gave it to the pipling, all the while staring into his yellow and red eyeballs. "But always remember: I AM IN CHARGE!"

"*Srrrrrr,*" trilled Worm.

Angus grinned. "Did you hear that, Wiggie? He called me 'Sir!'"

"I heard it." Wiglaf smiled. "Now tell him to get out of the moat, Angus. Or we'll catch our death of cold!"

After that, Worm followed Angus back to the henhouse like a little duckling. The boys' uniforms were soaking wet and smelly from the moat. So they cut Scrub-a-Thon and hid out in the henhouse that afternoon. They kept busy with training Worm.

Even Daisy, who'd returned from the library with a big stack of books, was impressed with how fast the pipling learned. That very afternoon Angus taught Worm "Sit" and "Down." Sir Sitstayheel recommended training with both hand signals and English commands.

Over the next few days, they worked with the pipling between Scrub-a-Thon chores, until he had nailed "Stay," "Come," and "Leave it," "Give a paw," "Speak" and "No speak!" He loved playing games, so Wiglaf taught him Fetch and Hide & Seek. But the Pipling's favorite game was one he made up himself. Wiglaf called it Make Me Laugh. Worm played it by making faces and doing silly things until the boys cracked up.

All this time, Worm was growing. Now the top of his little crested head came up to Wiglaf's shoulder.

That same night, just before torches out, Erica came over and sat on Wiglaf's cot. He had hardly seen her lately. She was either out on Dawn Patrol or doing extra-credit scrubbing.

"Dawn Patrol is over," Erica said. "Bragwort and I have finished carting Frypot's garbage heap to the trash pit."

"That whole mountain of garbage is gone?" said Angus.

Erica nodded proudly. "And how is that 'something' doing? The 'something' I don't know anything about?"

"He's fine," said Wiglaf. "Angus is very good at training the 'something.'"

Angus grinned. "If you can make eye contact, you can get a dragon to do anything you want."

"Eye contact?" Erica said. "I'll remember that." Then she looked puzzled. "Wiggie, what happened to your blanket?"

"'Something' needed a bed," said Wiglaf.

Erica ran off. When she returned, she was carrying a nice thick blanket and a pillow.

"You know me," she said. "I have extra everything." She plopped them down on Wiglaf's cot.

That night, Wiglaf felt warm and happy. He had never slept on a pillow before, and he felt as if he were floating on a cloud. He closed his eyes and fell asleep, smiling.

Soon Wiglaf was dreaming about Worm, calling, "*Mmmmommy! Mmmmommy!*"

Wiglaf rolled over in his sleep. He found himself pressed up against something hard and lumpy. Wiglaf opened one eye. A pair of yellow eyes stared back at him.

"*Mmmmmmommy!*" Worm cooed as he snuggled close to Wiglaf. He licked his face.

Wiglaf sat up. This was no dream. This was real! Worm had crawled into bed with him! Leaving Worm in the henhouse wasn't working. He couldn't stay in the dorm—he might be discovered. Was there anywhere outside? No. What if Worm decided to plunge into the moat again? Who knew what he'd think of next?

"Worm!" groaned Wiglaf. "What am I going to do with you?"

"*Mmmmmmommy!*" Worm burbled sleepily. "*Mmmmm.*"

Wiglaf couldn't help smiling. He closed his eyes and pulled Erica's thick warm blanket up to his chin. He'd figure it out tomorrow.

Chapter 7

BANG! BONG! BANG! BONG! BANG!

"Up and at 'em, Class I lads!" Frypot called. He banged on a skillet with his soup ladle.

Wiglaf's eyes popped open. He started to jump out of bed. Then he caught sight of the pointy green head sharing his pillow.

Worm's eyes lit up when he saw that Wiglaf was awake. He let out a joyful, "*Mmmmommy!*"

Wiglaf clapped a hand over the dragon's snout. He pulled the blanket over both their heads. Now what?

"Wiggie?" said Angus. "Are you awake?"

"Yes," said Wiglaf from under the covers. "But—I think—I will stay in bed for a while."

"Why? Are you sick?" said Angus.

"Sort of," said Wiglaf. He dared not say what the real trouble was.

"I bet you're faking it," said Bragwort. "To get out of scrubbing."

"Do you have a fever?" asked Angus.

"No," said Wiglaf. "I—I have a worm."

"Oh, no!" called Erica. "Have you eaten any uncooked eel, Wiggie?"

"No . . ." said Wiglaf.

"But why do you think you have a . . ." Angus drew in a sharp breath. "A—a worm?"

Wiglaf smiled. Angus got it now. He could tell.

"I'll get the de-worming tonic from Frypot," said Erica.

"I'm coming with you!" Bragwort called. "You're not getting a First Aid Badge unless I get one, too."

Wiglaf heard their footsteps as they raced out the door.

"My cousin had a worm in his stomach

once," Angus said. Wiglaf wondered why he was speaking so loudly. "One night the worm crawled out through his nose. It was six feet long!"

"Ewwwww!" cried several of the Class I boys.

Now Baldrick spoke up. "Can you catch worms?"

"Oh, yes," said Angus. "Worms are very contagious."

Wiglaf heard feet stampeding out of the dorm. Good old Angus!

When it was quiet, Angus drew back Wiglaf's blanket.

"*Srrrrrrr!*" Worm said happily.

"How in the world did he get up here?" asked Angus.

"Search me," said Wiglaf.

Worm hopped out of bed. "*Wrrrrrrm! Wrrrrrrrm!*"

The pipling had grown bigger yet. Wiglaf

saw that he was as tall as Angus!

"We have to get him out of here," Angus said. "Now!"

Just then the door opened.

Angus threw the blanket over the pipling to hide him. "Freeze!" he commanded.

Erica ran in.

Wiglaf breathed a sigh of relief.

"Here's the de-wormer," she said, holding up a bottle of dark brown syrup. When she saw the figure covered in her blanket, she stopped. "Don't tell me!" she said.

"We won't," said Angus.

"I don't see anything," said Erica. She squeezed her eyes shut. "But if I did, I'd think something has grown! And it's something that Bragwort—who's going to be back here in a minute—can't miss."

"Go head him off, Erica!" said Angus.

"Wait!" said Wiglaf. "Erica, if you have extra everything, does that include uniforms?"

Erica nodded. She kept her eyes shut. "Help yourself. They're in my trunk. Just don't step on my Sir Lancelot carpet, okay? I'm out of here." She turned and ran out the door.

In Erica's trunk, right on top, Wiglaf found a helmet, a freshly washed tunic and pair of leggings. "Angus," he said, "hold Worm still while I get him dressed."

Tucking Worm's tail into the leggings was a challenge, but ten minutes later, two DSA students holding one odd-looking creature in a DSA uniform between them left the Class I dorm room. They went right past Bragwort. Luckily, Erica had gotten him involved in counting his badges and he never looked up. As the three passed the headmaster's office, they heard the familiar *Clink! Clink!* Wiglaf breathed a sigh of relief. Mordred was busy counting his gold.

But to Wiglaf's horror, just as they had passed the suit of armor that stood guard out-

side the office, Mordred stuck his head out the door.

"Nephew!" he called, catching sight of Angus. "Tell me, what comes after 9,999?"

"Ten thousand, Uncle," answered Angus.

"Ah, I knew that! The inspectors. They've got me rattled, that's all." Mordred drew his head back in and slammed the door.

"*Wrrrrrrrm!*" Worm trilled. He bounced down the steps ahead of them. On the third bounce, Worm's wings ripped through Erica's tunic. The pipling began flapping, and bouncing higher and higher. And on a very high bounce, he kept flapping and stayed in the air.

"He's flying!" cried Angus.

"Sort of," said Wiglaf. "Good thing we put that helmet on him."

They watched as Worm took a nose dive onto the ground; then up he went again. This time he flew to Old Blodgett. He made a wobbly landing on the tree above the practice dragon's head.

"*Mmmmmmmmmommy! Srrrrrrr!*" Worm cried happily.

"Nice going!" called Angus, sounding like a proud parent. "Now <u>come</u>!"

"*Srrrrrrrr!*" Worm cried. Then he took off from the tree and flapped toward Angus. He bounced a few times then skidded right to him.

"Good, Worm," said Angus, tossing him an eel.

Angus and Wiglaf took the pipling to the henhouse door. Worm bounced inside.

"*Orry-say!*" Daisy cried. She told Wiglaf that she woke up that morning to find Worm gone and that he was too much for her to handle.

"Come on Daisy," said Angus. "No one ever comes to the henhouse."

"But Worm doesn't stay in the henhouse," Wiglaf pointed out. "Bragwort is suspicious. If he sees Worm, he'll tattle on us to Mordred.

You don't want that to happen."

"I'll show Uncle Mordred how well trained Worm is," said Angus. "He'll let me keep him as a pet."

"Dream on!" said Wiglaf. "We have to come up with a better plan than that!"

"Let's go get some breakfast," said Angus. "I can't think on an empty stomach."

No sooner had the boys sat down at the Class I table with their breakfast trays than Wiglaf caught sight of a huge rat peering in the dining-hall door. He had never known rats could reach such a size. Mordred looked up from where he sat at the teachers' table.

"Egad!" the headmaster cried. He jumped up from his chair and began waving the rat away. "Begone! Begone, I say! If the inspectors come and find a rat here, they'll close me down for sure!"

"No, lord," cried the rat "It's I, your scout, Yorick." He pulled off his rubbery rat's face.

"I knew that." Mordred mopped the sweat from his brow with the hem of his velvet cape. "These inspections have me on edge, that's all. Well, what news, Yorick?"

"My lord, the inspectors have just left Knights Noble Conservatory," said Yorick. "The school passed inspection with flying colors. Seems they got extra points for giving their students free time to work on their own projects."

"Free time?" muttered Mordred. "Never heard of it."

"The inspectors will go to Knights R Us tomorrow," said Yorick. "Then they are coming to Dragon Slayers' Academy." Yorick scratched his head. "Or is it the other way around?"

Mordred rolled his violet eyes. "In any case, we must be ready!" he boomed. "You boys have scrubbed well."

The boys broke into cheers.

"Uh-oh," said Angus. "Uncle Mordred never gives compliments."

Wiglaf feared what was coming next.

"But from now until the inspectors come," Mordred went on, "you shall scrub as you have never scrubbed before!"

Now the boys groaned.

"So! I've got new badges!" Mordred held up a bright red patch. It was decorated with feathers. "Who wants to earn this handsome badge?"

"The fancier the badge . . ." said Wiglaf.

"The nastier the job," Angus finished.

As Mordred swung the fancy badge back and forth, Wiglaf glanced out the window and nearly choked on his eel. There was Worm! The pipling was flapping his wings, treading air. When he saw that Wiglaf had seen him, he wiggled his ears.

"Angus!" Wiglaf elbowed him and nodded toward the window.

"Lancelot's liver!" Angus swore. He frowned at the pipling, nodding at him to go away.

But Worm only frowned and nodded in imitation.

Wiglaf's mind was spinning. They had to get Worm away from there before anyone saw him. He stared down at his Eel-meal. And the disgusting gray glop gave him an answer. Wiglaf jumped up. "I'm going to be sick!" he cried. He clapped a hand over his mouth, and raced from the dining hall.

"I'll help you, Wiggie!" Angus called. And he ran after Wiglaf.

The boys zoomed out of the castle and into the yard.

"Worm!" called Angus. "Get down here!"

The pipling swooped down toward the boys. But at the last minute, he swerved away and flew straight into the castle.

The boys ran back into the entryway.

Mordred's portrait lay on the floor. Pieces of armor were scattered everywhere, a helmet here, a chain-mail boot there. The boys followed the path of destruction up the staircase and down the Hall of Fame.

"He's taken a bite out of Sir Ichabod's shoulder!" cried Wiglaf.

"Sir Herbert's shield is eaten!" said Angus.

"There he is!" said Wiglaf.

Worm sat at the end of the hallway. He was licking his claws as if just finishing a big messy meal. Wiglaf saw that the pedestal that had once held Mordred's bust was empty.

The dragon looked up as the boys ran toward him. "*Mmmmmmmommy! Sirrrrrr!*" he cried, and big soap bubbles floated out of his mouth and nose.

Suddenly a loud bellow split the air.

"Zounds!" cried Wiglaf. "Has a horribly wounded bull gotten into the school?"

"No," said Angus. "That's Uncle Mordred!"

Chapter 8

"I'll get the dunderheaded varlets who trashed my castle!" Mordred growled. "I will stretch 'em on the rack until they snap!"

Heavy footsteps sounded up the stairs!

Wiglaf swallowed.

Angus was trembling. "He's not in a very good mood."

"*Mmmmmmom?*" Worm's little crest flattened against his head in fear.

"Quick!" said Wiglaf. "Let's get Worm into the dorm room!"

Wiglaf found an eel bit in his pocket. He waved it in front of Worm who trotted after him. Wiglaf tossed the eel into the dorm room, waited for Worm to bounce inside, and then slammed the door shut. Just in time, too.

Mordred came storming down the hallway. His face was a frightening shade of red.

"Those castle-wrecking knaves can run but they can't hide! Not from me, Mordred the Marvelous." Mordred's glowing eyes lit upon the boys. "Nephew! Wiglaf! Why aren't you scrubbing?"

"We—we are looking for the varlets who trashed your castle, Uncle," said Angus.

"Ah! Good! Good!" Mordred nodded.

All of a sudden, a loud thump sounded inside the dorm room. Wiglaf's heart began to thump, too.

"Egad!" Mordred looked over his shoulder. "What was that?"

"What was what, Uncle?" said Angus as the thumping grew louder.

"That noise!" said Mordred.

"Noise?" said Angus. He turned to Wiglaf. "Did you hear a noise?"

"Noise?" said Wiglaf as something banged to the floor.

"That!" cried Mordred. "Surely you heard *that!*"

"What, Uncle?" Angus looked puzzled. "Do you think you heard something?"

Mordred's violet eyes bulged. His face turned pale. "Nephew! Are you suggesting that I am hearing things?"

"It is possible, Uncle," Angus said, looking concerned.

Then to Wiglaf's horror, the Class I dorm room door flew open. And there stood Worm! The pipling's eyes lit up when he saw the boys. He grinned, showing his pointy fang.

Mordred let out a large sigh. "The inspectors, the pressure," he said. "The wretched students who bring me no gold. The endless Scrub-a-Thon. And now this—this—wreckage! It would break any man." Worm began bouncing in the doorway.

Don't turn around, sir! Wiglaf chanted inside his head. *Just don't turn around!*

"You need rest, Uncle," said Angus.

Worm hooked his claws on his lips and pulled his mouth into a wide grin.

"A nap might help, sir," Wiglaf suggested.

"Let me walk you back to your office, Uncle." Angus took him by the elbow. "You could lie down on—"

Worm cried, "*Srrrrrrrr?*"

Mordred whipped his head. He froze as he stared at the pipling, who had crossed his eyes, stuck out his tongue and was wiggling his pink ears.

"Good King Ken's britches!" Mordred cried. "You see it, don't you, boy?"

"See what, Uncle?" said Angus.

Mordred's violet eyes circled once inside their sockets then the large headmaster sagged against the wall. "Hearing things," he mumbled. "Seeing things. Must lie down. Must rest.

Must pull self together." So saying, he staggered off down the hallway.

"*Wrrrrrrrm!*" crowed Worm, thinking he'd won whatever game he'd been playing.

Wiglaf and Angus shoved Worm into the dorm room.

"We were soooo lucky," said Angus.

"Oh no!" groaned Wiglaf. "Worm was making a nest."

Worm had stripped the blankets off all the cots and piled them in the middle of the room. Lots of cots had been over turned in the process. Erica's pillow was ripped. Feathers were everywhere.

"Wiggie?" said Angus. "What's that on Erica's Sir Lancelot rug?"

Wiglaf went to take a look. "Pipling poo!" he cried. "A big pile of it—right on Sir Lancelot's head!" Dr. Pluck had been right about that. Pew!

"Oh, man!" cried Angus. "Worm's cleaned

out my stash!" He shot the pipling a dirty look. "At least he didn't eat the marshmallows." But Worm only jumped up and down on Angus's cot, burbling, "*Mmmommy! Sirrrrr! Mmmommy! Sirrrrrr!*"

Wiglaf figured this was as good a time as any to bring up what he'd been thinking about. "Angus, it's time to take Worm back."

"No, we can keep him!" said Angus. "I'll train him not to wreck stuff. Besides, you were the one who wanted to raise a pipling."

"And we did!" said Wiglaf. "But we can't keep a huge dragon, Angus. Worm gets bigger every day. He can fly now. He can feed himself. He'll be fine."

Angus folded his arm across his chest. "Let's just get this mess cleaned up."

Angus gathered the blankets while Wiglaf worked on getting the poo out of Erica's carpet. Even Worm helped by turning the cots right side up again. Wiglaf Worm-sat while

Angus went to lunch. Angus stayed with him while Wiglaf went to supper. Then, just before the other boys were due back, Wiglaf and Angus tucked Worm into Wiglaf's bed.

Angus covered the pipling with his blanket.

The pipling looked up at him. "*Sirrrrrr?*"

"I'm going to tell you a bedtime story, Worm," Wiglaf said. "Once upon a time there was a purple egg."

Worm murmured "*Mmmmmommy . . .*" He closed his eyes.

"Two boys found the egg and took it back to their school," Wiglaf went on. "And—"

"Out you came, Worm!" said Angus.

Worm's eyes popped open. "*Wrrrrrrrrrrm!*"

"Out came a pipling," Angus went on. "He was no bigger than a little bunny. The boys took good care of him. And the pipling grew and grew and grew."

The boys heard faint snoring sounds. Worm was blowing little soap bubbles from his nose. Now, except for the long, green snout, the dragon looked like any sleeping DSA student. Angus pulled the blanket up just over his head.

"At last the pipling grew too big to stay at the school," Wiglaf picked up the story even though Worm was fast asleep. He looked straight at Angus as he spoke. "So the boys took him back to the Dark Forest. The pipling flew off. He found other dragons to play with, and lived happily ever after."

The pipling smiled in his sleep. He murmured a faint, "*Haaa haaa!*"

Angus sighed. "You win," he said. "We'll take him back tonight."

After all the Class I boys were sound asleep, Wiglaf rolled out from under Angus's cot, where he'd been hiding. Angus woke Worm. And the three of them made their quiet way out of DSA.

"I hope Worm won't be scared in the forest," said Angus as they walked through the starlit night.

Worm bounced along happily between them. Every once in a while, he spread his wings and flew part of the way. At last, they reached the bank of the Swamp River.

"Snack time!" said Angus. He pulled two marshmallows from his pocket, stuck them on a stick and held them out to Worm. "Flame up!" he said.

Whoosh! Worm toasted them until they were perfect—crispy, but not burned. The boys were licking marshmallow goo off their fingers, when they heard a strange noise. "*Haaa haaaa haaa!*"

"What is that?"

Now Worm spread his wings, and answered: "*Haaa haaaa haaa!*"

Wiglaf heard flapping wings. He and Angus

hunkered down. Out of the dark, a pair of piplings came flying down. They looked just like Worm. Except that they had purple ears. And they were a little bigger.

"Worm's sisters!" whispered Wiglaf. "I guess Worm was the runt."

The three piplings bounced around, circling each other. They took turns shooting flames from their noses. They hooted their wild cry. Wiglaf knew he was seeing something that few had ever seen. He just hoped that he and Angus might live to tell about it.

Then Wiglaf's hair began blowing in the breeze as the piplings rose into the air. They circled once over Wiglaf and Angus's heads.

"*Mmmmmmmommy! Sirrrrrrrrrrrrrrrrr!*" called Worm. He glided down to the boys. He crossed his eyes, stuck out his tongue, and wiggled his ears. Then up he flew to join his sisters. And the three piplings disappeared over the Dark Forest.

Chapter 9

With heavy hearts, Wiglaf and Angus walked to Dr. Pluck's class. They didn't care if they were late and had to sit up front in the Spit Zone.

The boys didn't care about much of anything now that Worm was gone. Angus had lost his appetite. Wiglaf daydreamed during classes. Once, he thought he saw Worm winging through the sky. But it was only a crow.

St. Globule's Day had come and gone, but still the inspectors had not arrived. At last, Mordred realized there was nothing left to scrub or shine, so classes started up again.

Wiglaf and Angus reached Dr. Pluck's classroom and sat down in the front row. Wiglaf took his notebook from his tunic pocket. Then he saw that it wasn't his notebook at all. It was *97 Ways to Train Your Dragon*. Worm! He wondered how the pipling was doing in the wild.

"**Pu**pils!" Dr. Pluck rapped his pointer. "Who knows the **pro**per way to **p**rotect **p**eo**p**le from a **p**ack of dragons?"

Wiglaf held up *97 Ways to Train Your Dragon* to protect himself from the spray.

Just then the classroom door opened. Mordred swept in wearing his best red velvet cape. "Continue, Dr. Pluck," the headmaster said. "These gentlemen only want to see the high quality education that goes on each and every day here at Dragon Slayers' Academy."

"The inspectors!" Angus whispered.

A tall inspector, a short inspector, and a plump inspector followed Mordred into the classroom. They wore black robes. They carried parchment books. They peered at the students and scribbled in their books. They peered and scribbled in Sir Mort's Stalking Class. And again, in Coach Plungett's Slaying Class. Wiglaf thought the inspectors did not look pleased. Finally, lunchtime rolled around.

Wiglaf, Angus, and Erica sat together.

"Are you not hungry, Angus?" said Erica.

"Not really," said Angus. "I miss you know who."

"Worm is with his sisters," Wiglaf said. "He's happy."

"But I'm not," said Angus. "At last I find a pet who liked me. And now he's gone!"

Before lunch was over, Mordred stood up. "All right, lads. Off with you. It's free time!"

Free time? Wiglaf and Angus exchanged glances. What was Mordred talking about? There was never any free time.

"Our pupils love free time," Mordred told the inspectors. "That's when they do, well, you know, those free-time things."

Angus rolled his eyes while Wiglaf pulled
97 *Ways to Train Your Dragon* from his pocket.

"We have no more need of this," he said
sadly. "We can return it to the library during
free time."

Angus and Erica nodded. And after lunch
the three of them headed for the south tower.
Slowly, they climbed the steps.

Wiglaf opened the library door. "Brother
Dave?" he called. "I have come to return—" He
stopped dead in his tracks as a large something
sprang at him, burbling, "*Mmmmmmommy!
Mmmmmmommy!*"

"Worm?" Wiglaf blinked.

"Worm!" Angus shouted. He threw his
arms around the dragon's middle.

"How did he get here?" cried Erica.

"He flewest in through an open window
some time ago," said Brother Dave. "As thou
knowest, Daisy cometh up here daily. She

hadst told me of yon pipling. And how Wiglaf and Angus had tamed and trained him well."

Wiglaf smiled. Good old Daisy!

Footsteps sounded on the stairs. Students with free time, coming to the library! Wouldn't Brother Dave be thrilled?

"'Tis good I hadst opened yon window," Brother Dave was saying. "I hadst wished to air out the library before the inspectors—"

"Inspectors!" cried Wiglaf. "I hear them!"

"The last stop on our tour is the li-berry," Mordred was saying as he led the inspectors up the last few stairs.

"Library," the tall inspector corrected him.

"Of course!" said Mordred. "We have lots of . . . of those things that are kept in libraries."

"Books," said the plump inspector. "They are called books."

Erica tried to shove Worm toward the window. "Fly! Bye-bye! Go, on! Scat!"

But Worm thought Erica was playing a

game. He started bouncing around the library.

"Angus! Do something!" said Wiglaf.

Angus stepped forward. "Worm!" he commanded. "Come!"

A second later, the library door opened.

"Yoo-hoo, Brother Dan?" called Mordred. "I have brought some important visitors to see the lib—er, the room up here."

Brother Dave stood behind his desk. "Thou art welcome, sirs," he said. "One and all."

Wiglaf's heart pounded as the three inspectors trooped in.

Mordred and the inspectors saw bright sunlight streaming in through big windows. They saw rows and rows of books. They saw one student lounging on a big stuffed unicorn pillow. Two others were lounging on a dragon pillow. At least, it seemed to be a pillow. All three were reading books.

The tall inspector smiled down at Wiglaf. "So students come here to read in their

free time."

Wiglaf looked up from his book. "Yes, sir," he said. "We do."

"Excuse us for a moment," said the tall inspector. Then the three huddled together. At last, they raised their heads.

"Headmaster Mordred!" the tall inspector said. "By rights, we should close you down."

Mordred clasped his hands together. "No, kind sirs!" he cried. "Say not so!"

"The food is disgusting," the tall inspector continued. "The dormitories are freezing. Most of your teachers are halfwits!"

"True," said Mordred. "But—"

"Shhh!" The plump inspector cut him off. "But this library is a wonderful sight! It is the reason—the only reason—that we will recommend that DSA stay open."

Then the inspectors filed out of the library.

Mordred hurried after them. "So I'm still in business. Is that what you're saying? I've passed inspection? I knew it! Now, how much can I raise the tuition?"

When the door closed behind them, there was much rejoicing in the DSA library.

"DSA forever!" cried Erica.

"Worm!" said Angus giving the "pillow" a great big hug. "You're going to stay here forever."

"Well, Angus the truth is that the pipling cometh and goeth from this tower as he pleases," Brother Dave explained. "When he ist here, I am glad of his company, for as Daisy sayeth, he is a pipling who loves a good book." He patted the dragon proudly on the head. "Thou art my book Worm!"

Worm purred and grinned.

Wiglaf smiled. How glad he was that he'd brought that purple egg to DSA.

THE END

The Campus of Dragon Slayers' Academy

DSA

Lady Lobelia's Chamber

Dr. Pluck's Science Lab

Mordred's Classroom

Tun Exi

Headmaster's Office

Sta

Ca Ya

Dining Hall

To Dungeon

Scrubbing Class

Prac Dra

Yorick's Quick Change-O-Rama Camp site

~ Our Founders ~

Sir Herbert Dungeonstone

Sir Ichabod Popquiz

Sir Herbert and Sir Ichabod founded DSA on a simple principle still held dear: Any lad—no matter how weak, yellow-bellied, lazy, pigeon-toed, smelly, or unwilling—can be transformed into a fearless dragon slayer. After four years at DSA, lads will finally be of some worth to their parents, as well as a source of great wealth to this distinguished academy.* ** ***

* Please note that Dragon Slayers' Academy is a strictly-for-profit institution.

** Dragon Slayers' Academy reserves the right to keep some of the gold and treasure that any student recovers from a dragon's lair.

*** The exact amount of treasure given to a student's family is determined solely by our esteemed headmaster, Mordred. The amount shall be no less than 1/500th of the treasure and no greater than 1/499th.

～ Our Headmaster ～

Mordred de Marvelous

Mordred graduated from Dragon Bludgeon High, second in his class. The other student, Lionel Flyzwattar, went on to become headmaster of Dragon Stabbers' Prep. Mordred spent years as part-time, semi-substitute student teacher at Dragon Whackers' Alternative School, all the while pursuing his passion for mud wrestling. Inspired by how filthy rich Flyzwattar had become by running a school, Mordred founded Dragon Slayers' Academy in CMLXXIV, and has served as headmaster ever since.

❧

Known to the Boys as: Mordred de Miser
Dream: Piles and piles of dragon gold
Reality: Yet to see a single gold coin
Best-Kept Secret: Mud wrestled under the name Macho-Man Mordie
Plans for the Future: Will retire to the Bahamas . . . as soon as he gets his hands on a hoard

~ Our Faculty ~

Sir Mort du Mort

Sir Mort is our well-loved professor of Dragon Slaying. In his youth, he was known as the Scourge of Dragons. Sir Mort's last encounter was with the most dangerous dragon of them all: Knight-shredder. Early in the battle, Sir Mort took a nasty blow to his helmet and has never been the same since.

Coach Wendell Plungett

Coach Plungett spent many years questing in the Dark Forest before joining the Athletic Department. When he left his dragon-slaying days behind him, Coach Plungett was the manliest man to be found anywhere north of Nowhere Swamp. "I am what you call a hunk," the coach admits.

~ Faculty ~

Brother Dave

Brother Dave is the DSA librarian. He belongs to the Little Brothers of the Peanut Brittle, an order known for doing impossibly good deeds and cooking up endless batches of peanut candy. After a batch of his extra-crunchy peanut brittle left three children toothless, Brother Dave vowed to do a truly impossible good deed. Thus did he offer to be librarian at a school world-famous for considering reading and writing a complete and utter waste of time.

Professor Prissius Pluck

Professor Pluck graduated from Peter Piper Picked a Peck of Pickled Peppers Prep, and went on to become a professor of science at Dragon Slayers' Academy. Boys who take Dragon Science, Professor Pluck's popular class, are amazed at the great quantities of saliva Professor P. can project and try never to sit in the front row.

Frypot

How Frypot came to be the cook at DSA is something of a mystery. Rumors abound. Some say that when Mordred bought the broken-down castle for his school, Frypot was already in the kitchen. Others say Frypot knows many a dark secret that keeps him from losing his job. But no one ever, *ever* says that Frypot was hired because he can cook.

Yorick

Yorick is Chief Scout at DSA and a master of disguise. His knack for masquerading as almost anything comes from his years with the Merry Minstrels and Dancing Damsels Players, where he won an award for his role as the Glass Slipper in "Cinderella".

Wiglaf of Pinwick

Wiglaf, our newest lad, hails from a hovel outside the village of Pinwick, which makes Toenail look like a thriving metropolis. Being one of thirteen children, Wiglaf had a taste of dorm life before coming to DSA and he fit right in. He started the year off with a bang when he took a stab at Coach Plungett's brown pageboy wig. Way to go, Wiggie! We hope to see more of this lad's wacky humor in the years to come.

⚜

Dream: Bold Dragon-Slaying Hero
Reality: Still hangs on to a "security" rag
Extracurricular Activities: Animal-Lovers Club, President; No More Eel for Lunch Club, President; Frypot's Scrub Team, Brush Wielder; Pig Appreciation Club, Founder
Favorite Subject: Library
Oft-Heard Saying: *"Ello-hay, Aisy-day!"*
Plans for the Future: To go for the gold!

Eric von Royale

Eric hails from Someplace Far Away (at least that's what he wrote on his Application Form). There's an air of mystery about this Class I lad, who says he is "totally typical and absolutely average." If that is so, how did he come to own the rich tapestry that hangs over his cot? And are his parents really close personal friends of Sir Lancelot? Did Frypot the cook bribe him to start the Clean Plate Club? And doesn't Eric's arm ever get tired from raising his hand in class so often?

❧

Dream: Valiant Dragon Slayer
Reality: Teacher's Pet
Extracurricular Activities: Sir Lancelot Fan Club; Armor Polishing Club; Future Dragon Slayer of the Month Club; DSA Pep Squad, Founder and Cheer Composer
Favorite Subject: All of Them!!!!!
Oft-Heard Saying: *"When I am a mighty Dragon Slayer . . ."*
Plans for the Future: To take over DSA

Angus du Pangus

The nephew of Mordred and Lady Lobelia, Angus walks the line between saying, "I'm just one of the lads" and "I'm going to tell my uncle!" Will this Class I lad ever become a mighty dragon slayer? Or will he take over the kitchen from Frypot some day? We of the DSA Yearbook staff are betting on choice #2. And hey, Angus? The sooner the better!

❧

Dream: A wider menu selection at DSA
Reality: Eel, Eel, Eel!
Extracurricular Activities: DSA Cooking Club, President; Smilin' Hal's Off -Campus Eatery, Sales Representative
Favorite Subject: Lunch
Oft-Heard Saying: *"I'm still hungry"*
Plans for the Future: To write *101 Ways to Cook a Dragon*

Baldrick de Bold

This is a banner year for Baldrick. He is celebrating his tenth year as a Class I lad at DSA. Way to go, Baldrick! If any of you new students want to know the ropes, Baldrick is the one to see. He can tell when you should definitely *not* eat the cafeteria's eel, where the choice seats are in Professor Pluck's class, and what to tell the headmaster if you are late to class. Just don't ask him the answer to any test questions.

⚜

Dream: To run the world
Reality: A runny nose
Extracurricular Activities: Practice Dragon Maintenance Squad; Least Improved Slayer-in-Training Award
Favorite Subject: *"Could you repeat the question?"*
Oft Heard Saying: *"A dragon ate my homework."*
Plans for the Future: To transfer to Dragon Stabbers' Prep